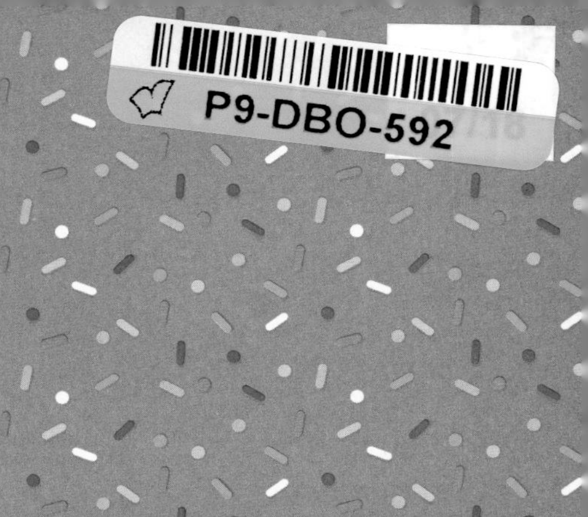
P9-DBO-592

 Published in the United States by Random House Children's Books, a division of Penguin Random House LLC, 1745 Broadway, New York, NY 10019, and in Canada by Penguin Random House Canada Limited, Toronto. Beginner Books, Random House, and the Random House colophon are registered trademarks of Penguin Random House LLC.

Visit us on the Web!
rhcbooks.com

Educators and librarians, for a variety of teaching tools, visit us at RHTeachersLibrarians.com.

Library of Congress Cataloging-in-Publication Data
Names: Lewman, David, author. | Laguna, Fabio, illustrator. | Mills, Grace, illustrator. | DreamWorks Animation.
Title: Too many cupcakes! / by David Lewman ; illustrated by Fabio Laguna and Grace Mills.
Other titles: Adaptation of (expression): Trolls (Motion picture)
Description: First edition. | New York : Random House, [2018] | Series: Dreamworks Trolls | Series: Beginner books
Identifiers: LCCN 2017047081 | ISBN 978-0-525-57800-0 (hardback) | ISBN 978-0-525-57801-7 (lib. bdg.) | ISBN 978-0-525-57802-4 (ebook)
Subjects: | BISAC: JUVENILE FICTION / Media Tie-In. | JUVENILE FICTION / Readers / Beginner. | JUVENILE FICTION / Action & Adventure / General.
Classification: LCC PZ7.L5894 Too 2018 | DDC [E]—dc23
LC record available at https://lccn.loc.gov/2017047081

Printed in the United States of America
10 9 8 7 6 5 4 3 2 1
First Edition

TOO MANY CUPCAKES!

By David Lewman
Illustrated by Fabio Laguna and Grace Mills

BEGINNER BOOKS®
Random House New York

There are many kinds of Trolls.
Biggie is the tallest Troll.
Mr. Dinkles is his pet worm.

Biggie and Mr. Dinkles
bake sweet treats.

Poppy comes to visit.
Poppy needs cupcakes.
LOTS of cupcakes!
She needs them
for a party.

Biggie gets to work.
He pours the flour
into two big bowls.

Biggie mixes . . .

and mixes . . .

and mixes

the batter.

It goes everywhere!

What a mess.

Baking so many cupcakes
is too much work
for one Troll.

Biggie goes to find help.

But the other Trolls
are getting ready
for Poppy's party, too.

They are too busy
to help bake.

Biggie sees Cloud Guy
in the forest.
Biggie tells him his problem.
Cloud Guy has an idea.

Bizzy Buzzer Bugs
love to work hard.
Biggie should ask them
if they want to help.

Biggie asks the bugs.

The bugs would
LOVE to help!

Biggie shows the bugs
how to make cupcakes.
They mix the batter.

They pour the batter.

They put the pans
in the oven.

They take the cupcakes
out of the oven.

The bugs decorate
the cupcakes.
They use ALL
the sprinkles.

Biggie leaves
to get some more.

While Biggie is gone,
the bugs keep making cupcakes.
LOTS of cupcakes!

Cupcakes fill
the bakery!

Cupcakes spill out
of the bakery!

Cupcakes fill the paths!

Cupcakes fill the homes!

Cupcakes fill
THE WHOLE VILLAGE!

Biggie returns
with the sprinkles.
Oh, no. . . .

THERE ARE
TOO MANY
CUPCAKES!

Cloud Guy waves to Biggie.

"Bizzy Buzzer Bugs
are very good workers,"
says Cloud Guy.
"But they are not
very good at stopping."

"Thank you
for your help!"
Biggie tells the bugs.
"You can stop now."

The bugs go home.
They had fun
making cupcakes.

Poppy invites Bridget
to her big party.
She loves Biggie's cupcakes.
Bridget and the Trolls
eat them ALL!

The next day,
Biggie goes back
to baking.
This time, he does it
all by himself–
except for Mr. Dinkles.

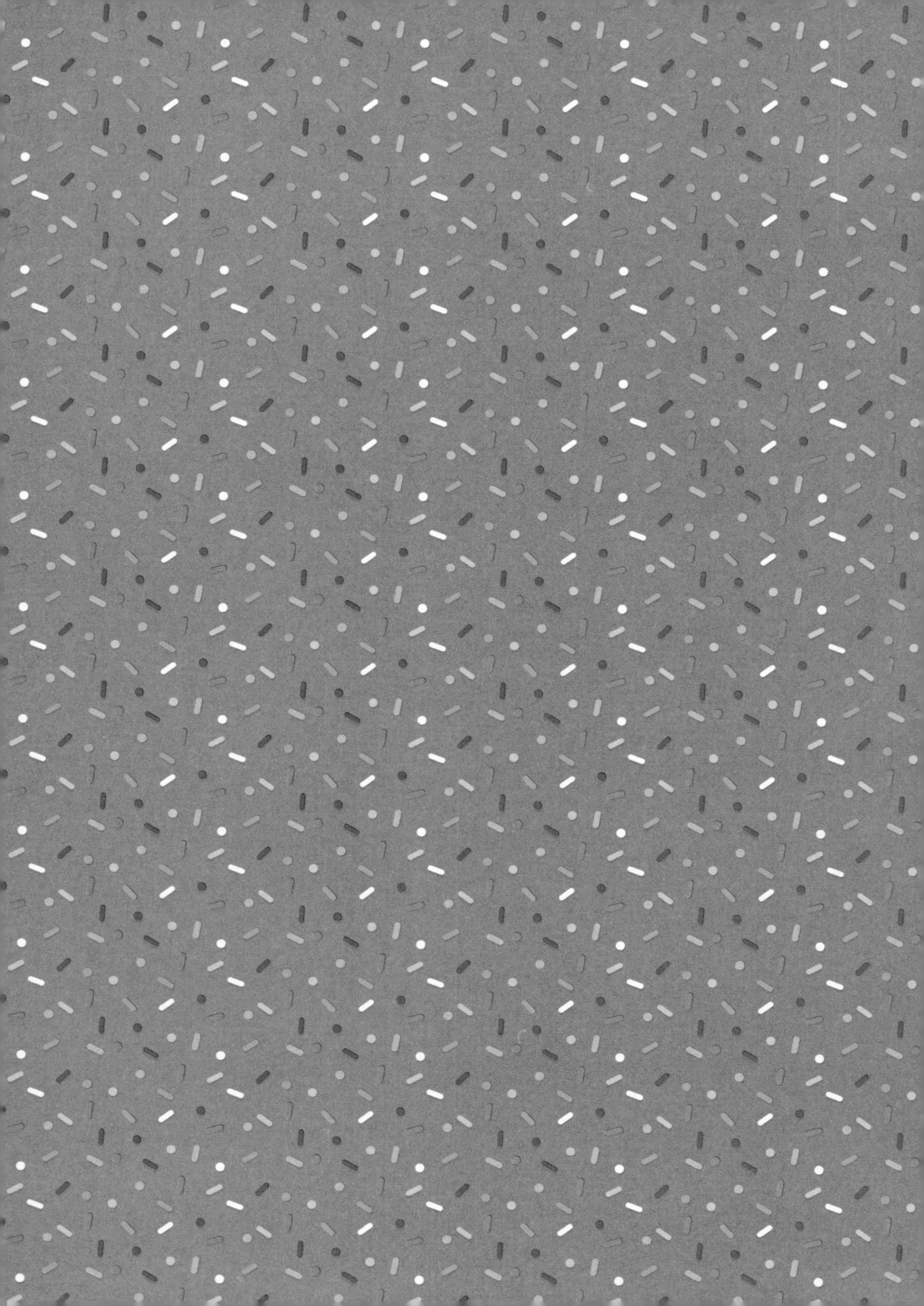